Zoe's Rescue ZOO

The Scruffy Sea Otter

Amelia Cobb

Illustrated by **Sophy Williams**

nosy crow

With special thanks to Natalie Doherty

To Theo

First published in the UK in 2017 by Nosy Crow Ltd
The Crow's Nest, 10a Lant St
London, SE1 1QR, UK

Nosy Crow and associated logos are trademarks and/or
registered trademarks of Nosy Crow Ltd

Text copyright © Hothouse Fiction, 2017
Illustrations copyright © Sophy Williams, 2017

The right of Hothouse Fiction and Sophy Williams to be identified as the author
and illustrator respectively of this work has been asserted by them in accordance
with the Copyright, Designs and Patents Act 1988.

Printed and bound in the UK by Clays Ltd, St Ives Plc

Papers used by Nosy Crow are made from wood grown in sustainable forests.

ISBN: 978 085763 847 2

www.nosycrow.com

Chapter One
A Monday Morning Mystery

"Brrrriiing! Brrrriiing!"

Zoe Parker's eyes flew open as the telephone rang downstairs. It was still very early in the morning, and Zoe could tell from the dim light coming through her curtains that the sun hadn't properly come up yet.

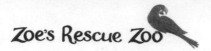

"Who's calling so early?" she mumbled, rubbing her eyes.

Usually on school days Zoe was woken by the sound of Oscar the African elephant trumpeting noisily in his enclosure! That was because Zoe lived somewhere very special: the Rescue Zoo.

The Rescue Zoo was an amazing place where animals who had no home or who were lost or hurt could find a safe place to live. Zoe's great-uncle, Horace Higgins, had started the zoo several years ago. He was a famous animal expert and explorer, and he was off on one of his adventures around the world right now.

Zoe's mum, Lucy, was the Rescue Zoo's vet, and she and Zoe lived in a cosy little cottage on the edge of the zoo. This meant that Zoe could visit the animals any time she wanted! Zoe thought she was the luckiest girl in the world to live where she did. She loved animals more than anything!

As the telephone continued to ring, Zoe heard her mum's bedroom door creak open and footsteps pad downstairs. "Hello?" she heard her mum say sleepily.

Suddenly Zoe had a thought. "Meep, are you awake?" she whispered anxiously. "I hope one of the animals isn't poorly!"

Zoe knew that the night keepers would ring Lucy in an animal emergency, no matter what time it was, so that her mum could rush out and help.

There was silence for a moment. Then, at the foot of the bed, next to Zoe's toes, the duvet cover wriggled. A little furry face with big golden eyes popped out!

Meep was a grey mouse lemur with soft fur and a long curly tail. He was Zoe's best friend and he lived in the cottage with Zoe and her mum. Zoe and Meep did everything together – including talking!

On her sixth birthday, Zoe had realised that she could understand animals' grunts, barks and roars, and speak back to them too. It had made living in the Rescue Zoo even more fun! Zoe had always kept this a secret from other people though – even her mum.

Meep's pointy ears were pricked up, so that he could listen to what Lucy was saying. Zoe knew that lemurs had excellent hearing – much better than humans'! "I think she's laughing, Zoe!" he chirped.

To Zoe's relief, she realised that Meep was right. She could hear now that Lucy was chatting happily with whoever was on the other end of the telephone. That must mean that none of the animals were hurt or ill. "So what do you think's going on, Meep?" she wondered.

Meep's ears twitched. "She's coming back up the stairs now," he squeaked. "Maybe we'll find out!"

Zoe heard footsteps on the stairs again,

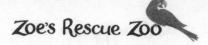
and a moment later there was a gentle
tap on Zoe's bedroom door.

"Zoe, are you awake?" asked Lucy,
popping her head inside the room. Zoe
and her mum had the same dark curly
hair and freckles. Lucy was beaming with
excitement. "I've got a surprise for you!"
she said. "Quick, hop out of bed and
come with me."

"What is it? Where are we going?"
asked Zoe, climbing out of bed.

"You'll see!" replied her mum. "Put
some clothes on and meet me downstairs."

Zoe stared as her mum disappeared
back into her own bedroom, humming
cheerily. "This is so weird!" she whispered
to Meep as she quickly put on some
clothes and laced up her trainers.

Meep jumped from the bed and perched

on her shoulder. "I'm coming too!" he
chattered eagerly.

Zoe and Meep were waiting by the
front door when Lucy appeared. She
smiled when she saw them. "Let's go!" she
said, ushering them outside and locking
the door behind them.

"Where are we going?" Zoe asked again. "What's happening?"

"You'll find out very soon, I promise," her mum assured her.

To Zoe's surprise, her mum walked towards the Jeep that was parked round the side of the cottage and got in.

Zoe climbed into the Jeep and strapped herself in, with Meep nestling in her lap. Lucy started the engine and they began to drive slowly through the zoo. The early morning sun was casting a warm light over the flowerbeds bursting with spring flowers and the tall rooftops of Higgins Hall. This was the huge manor house that had belonged to Great-Uncle Horace's family for years and years, and was now home to some of the Rescue Zoo's reptiles.

Lots of the animals were beginning to
stir as Zoe and her mum drove along.
The giraffes were stretching out their long
necks, just like Zoe always stretched her
arms in the morning, and the hippos were
plodding into their mud bath for an early

morning dip. But Zoe spotted the owls
cuddling together on a branch in their
enclosure with their eyes starting to close.
Most of them were nocturnal animals,
just like bats, which meant they slept
through the daytime instead of at night.

Zoe smiled to see Rory, the little lion cub, yawn widely and stretch out his paws before nudging his friend Leonard awake. As the Jeep rumbled past the lions' enclosure, Zoe saw Rory stare at them in surprise and growl curiously. The little cub wanted to know where Zoe was off to in the early hours of the morning – almost as much as Zoe herself did!

"I love seeing the zoo like this!" Zoe said. "It's so quiet without any visitors."

Lucy nodded. "This is one of my favourite times of day too, when the only people around are the zoo keepers."

Just as she said this, Zoe spotted Jess, the otter keeper, walking along the path in the direction of the otter enclosure. Her blonde hair was tied back in a plait and she was carrying a big red bucket of fish.

"Jess must be about to give the otters their breakfast!" Zoe said, waving.

They drove right through the zoo and out of the gates, which were carved from wood and showed lots of different animals. Zoe frowned as she noticed which road her mum was taking them down. "We're heading towards the river!" she realised.

"That's right," said her mum, grinning.

Zoe was beginning to feel very excited – and *very* curious!

The Jeep turned a corner and as the river came into view Zoe saw a boat in the distance, sailing towards them. It was bright red, with a yellow sail fluttering in the breeze. Painted on the sail was a symbol: a colourful hot-air balloon. Zoe could make out a figure standing at the

13

wheel, with a head of untidy white hair. As she watched, the figure raised an arm and waved.

Zoe stared. "That's the Rescue Zoo boat!" she cried. "And … that's Great-Uncle Horace! He's back!"

Chapter Two
First Mate Zoe!

Zoe bounced up and down impatiently
in her seat as her mum parked the Jeep.
As soon as the engine had been switched
off she unbuckled her seat belt, scooped
Meep into her arms, jumped out of the
Jeep and raced to the river's edge, waving.
"Great-Uncle Horace!" she shouted
excitedly.

Chuckling, her mum joined her. "It was Great-Uncle Horace on the phone this morning!" she explained. "He thought this would be a fun surprise."

The boat drew closer to the riverbank and Zoe saw Great-Uncle Horace throw out a long rope, which Lucy caught and wrapped tightly around a wooden post. Great-Uncle Horace was wearing a tattered, stripy sailor's jumper and a blue captain's hat, and his white beard looked even wilder than usual. "All aboard!" he called, beaming as the boat bumped against the bank. "Take my hand, First Mate Zoe, and hop on!"

Zoe reached out her hand, grabbed Great-Uncle Horace's and jumped aboard the boat, with Lucy just behind her. It felt strange and wobbly underneath

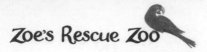

her feet, and she had to take a few steps to find her balance. Meep squealed anxiously and scrambled on to her shoulder, wrapping his long tail around her neck to make sure he didn't fall off.

"Great-Uncle Horace, I've really missed you!" Zoe cried, jumping into his arms for a hug. "You've been gone for ages this time."

"And I'm so happy to be home, Zoe!"

Great-Uncle Horace replied warmly. "I've been on such an adventure. I've been to Russia! It's such a vast country, full of huge mountains, wild forests – and lots of different animals that needed my help! Isn't that right, Kiki?"

There was a squawk as a blue bird fluttered down from the flagpole and landed on Great-Uncle Horace's shoulder. Kiki was a hyacinth macaw with beautiful glossy feathers, bright, beady eyes and a curved beak. Great-Uncle Horace had rescued her when she was only an egg, and she'd stayed with him ever since.

"It's been a long journey back!" continued Great-Uncle Horace, stroking Kiki fondly.

"Did you find an animal who needed

19

a place to live?" asked Zoe hopefully. Whenever Great-Uncle Horace came across an animal that couldn't stay in the wild any more, he brought them back to the Rescue Zoo. Zoe's mind whirled as she thought about some of the creatures who had arrived at the zoo recently: a gorgeous family of arctic wolves; a pair of cheeky panda cubs; a fluffy baby polar bear. If Great-Uncle Horace *had* brought a new animal back this time, what would it be?

Great-Uncle Horace laughed. "I certainly did, Zoe," he replied. "Not just one animal — but *three*! Take a look inside that crate."

Zoe turned and saw a large wooden crate tucked securely at the back of the boat. She stepped towards it and peered through a gap between the wooden boards. All she could make out were three sets of dark, shining eyes. On her shoulder, Meep gave an excited squeak.

"I can't tell what they are!" Zoe cried.

"Let me give you a clue," said Great-Uncle Horace. "These animals are mammals, but they spend lots of time in the water."

Zoe bit her lip and thought. "Polar bears?" she guessed. "Or maybe . . . seals!"

Great-Uncle Horace shook his head and gave a big smile. "They're sea otters!" he explained. "Baby otters are called pups, just like baby seals. There are two sisters and one brother. I'm afraid they were orphaned when Russian hunters captured their parents — sea otters are often hunted for their fur, which means they are an endangered species, sadly. So we'll give them a lovely, safe home at the Rescue Zoo."

"Otters!" said Zoe. "Like Otto and Benedict?"

"Well, Otto and Benedict are *river* otters, my dear," Great-Uncle Horace explained. "But these are *sea* otters. They need to live in saltwater, not freshwater. I've already sent a message to Jess, asking her to prepare a special area with a saltwater pool for our new arrivals to play in. I asked her to keep it a secret!"

"Jess *has* seemed very busy this week – and very mysterious!" said Lucy, laughing. "Now I know why."

"I bet that's where she was going when we saw her this morning – the new enclosure!" Zoe realised. "She'll be so excited to have three new baby otters to look after."

"Let's set off for the zoo right away," said Great-Uncle Horace. "Our new arrivals have travelled a long way, and they'll be tired and hungry. Perhaps you could help me with the crate, Lucy?"

Zoe jumped off the boat and watched as Great-Uncle Horace and her mum carefully lifted the crate off the boat and carried it to the boot of the Jeep. On the drive back to the zoo, Zoe listened to the snuffles and squeaks from inside the crate. When Lucy and Great-Uncle Horace were busy chatting in the front, she twisted round and whispered quietly, "Don't worry – we're going somewhere really lovely. I think you'll like it."

Once they reached the zoo, Lucy parked the Jeep right outside the new enclosure and they all jumped out. Jess was waiting by the gate, smiling. "Good morning!" she called. "Welcome back, Mr Higgins. I got your message about the new enclosure, and it's all ready. I can't wait to meet the pups!"

"I think that makes two of you!" replied Great-Uncle Horace, winking at Zoe,

who was grinning
excitedly.

The grown-ups
lifted the crate
out of the Jeep,
while Zoe
opened the
gate using
the necklace
she always wore.
It was a silver chain
with a charm shaped
like a paw print, which
contained a special chip that opened all
the gates and doors in the Rescue Zoo.
It had been her best-ever birthday present
from Great-Uncle Horace, and Zoe loved
it. She held the gate wide open as the
crate was carried inside and set down.

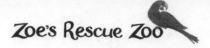

"You've done a marvellous job, Jess!"
exclaimed Great-Uncle Horace, and Jess
gave a big smile. Zoe thought so too.
There was a clear pool, with lots of big
wooden logs piled up around the edges,
and even some wooden ramps and slides
for the otters to play on. Dotted around
the edge of the enclosure were tall, leafy
trees that offered plenty of shade from
the sunshine. Waiting at the side of the
pool was the red bucket Zoe had seen Jess
carrying that morning, filled with shiny
fish for the otters to eat, and a pile of
colourful balls and other toys. "The water
is the perfect temperature for sea otters,
and there's just the right level of salt for
them," Jess explained.

Lucy unbuckled the straps on the crate
and gently lowered one side. Zoe held her

26

breath as there were high-pitched squeaks from inside the crate, and then a black snout appeared, sniffing the air. Next, a pale furry head, with whiskers and big, alert black eyes, followed by a sleek, dark body. The otter looked around at the enclosure, squeaked happily and trotted out of the crate.

"That's the oldest female," explained Great-Uncle Horace.

"She's so cute – and so small!" whispered Zoe.

A second otter followed straight after the first. "And that's her twin brother," added Great-Uncle Horace. "Otter twins are very rare, Zoe. I've never met a pair before. We're very lucky to have them! They're around a year old, I think."

Finally a third tiny face popped out

27

of the crate, glancing around shyly. This baby was even smaller than her sister and brother. Zoe gasped as the little otter scampered out. She had bright eyes and scruffy, tufty brown fur, sticking up in all directions. Zoe thought she was one of the most gorgeous things she'd ever seen! "That's the youngest pup, another female," Great-Uncle Horace explained. "Just four months old! And she's a little bit more nervous, so we'll need to make her feel extra welcome."

Zoe watched as the two older otters made straight for the edge of the water. "Oh no! What if they jump straight in?" she said anxiously. "Will they be OK?"

"Don't worry, Zoe," Great-Uncle Horace reassured her. "Baby otters are born knowing how to swim."

The otter twins plunged straight into
the water, gliding underneath the surface
before popping their heads back up and
squeaking excitedly. Their little sister
paused at the edge of the pool, watching
them eagerly, although she didn't look
as though she felt quite ready to follow
them. *As soon as she's settled in, I bet she'll be*

jumping in straight after them! Zoe thought.

"They love the water, don't they?" said Lucy, smiling as the twins splashed and ducked.

Zoe giggled. It seemed as though the new arrivals were feeling at home already!

Chapter Three
Zoe's Special Task

As Great-Uncle Horace, Lucy and Jess chatted about the otters' diet and what special supplies Jess would need, Zoe crouched down by the edge of the pool. She wanted to say hello to the otters and explain that she was there to help them with any problems or questions – and she was eager to make friends too! While the grown-ups were distracted, she decided to take her chance.

"I'm Zoe," she whispered, smiling at the twin otter pups, who looked at her curiously and then swam towards her. "I live here at the zoo, in a little cottage close by – my mum's the zoo vet, so her job is to take care of animals. And Meep lives here too. He's a grey mouse lemur and my best friend," she added.

Meep gave a friendly wave. "Hello! Welcome to the zoo," he chattered.

"What are your names?" asked Zoe.

The twins squealed back together, their eyes bright. "So you're Nina and you're Alex," repeated Zoe. "But how can I tell you apart? You look so alike."

Nina squeaked and waved a furry paw in the air, and Zoe spotted a patch of

paler fur. Glancing at Alex, Zoe saw that
her twin brother didn't have this extra
marking, and nodded. "That's a good way
to tell you apart!" she said. "And what's
your name?" she added, smiling at the
twins' little sister.

Shyly, the tiny otter squeaked her name.
"Sasha! What a pretty name," said Zoe.
"Meep and I really hope you like your
new home."

The twins squeaked eagerly, but
Zoe thought Sasha looked a little bit
bewildered. "Don't worry, Sasha. This is a
really nice place to live," Zoe whispered,
reaching out to stroke the pup. Unlike her
sleeker sister and brother, Sasha's fur was
tufty and fluffy, and stuck up messily. Zoe
thought she was so sweet!

Before she could say anything else,

Great-Uncle Horace, Jess and Lucy
walked over to join her. "Aren't they
fascinating creatures!" said Great-Uncle
Horace, beaming. "Did you know, Zoe,
that otters have the thickest fur in the

whole animal kingdom? Unfortunately that's why they're a target for hunters — their coats are wonderfully warm. They're very smart animals too — sea otters often use tools like pebbles or rocks to open shellfish, just as we might use a tin opener to open a tin!"

"Have you thought of names for them yet, Zoe?" Lucy asked.

Zoe smiled. She always tried to find out a new animal's name when they arrived at the zoo. Then, because she couldn't tell anyone that she had spoken to the animal, she often pretended she had thought of the name herself! "I thought we could call the twins Nina and Alex," she suggested shyly. "Nina has a light mark on one of her paws, so we can tell which twin is which. And can we call the little one Sasha?"

"I think those names are perfect," said Lucy.

Just as she said this, Sasha wriggled her body determinedly and plunged into the water with a splash. "She must have decided it was safe to give it a try!" Lucy laughed.

Zoe watched as Sasha paddled after her brother and sister, but she wasn't as fast as them and was struggling to keep up, despite squeaking hopefully at them to wait for her. The twins were floating on their backs close together, with their paws clasped, and didn't seem to notice their little sister. Great-Uncle Horace saw Zoe's anxious face and smiled reassuringly. "The twins have a very close bond," he explained. "That means their little sister

might get left out sometimes – but there's no need to worry, Zoe. We've just been discussing how to make sure she settles in just as well as her big sister and brother."

Jess nodded. "Because the otters are so young, I'll need to help encourage them to learn the important skills their mum would have shown them in the wild," she explained. "Things like using tools, diving for food, and becoming even better, faster swimmers. Sasha will need extra time and attention, though, because she's the smallest. So every day, I'll spend a few hours supporting her, until she can keep up with the twins."

Zoe's hand shot in the air. She didn't even have to think it over – she already knew this was something she wanted to assist with if she could! "Can I help?" she pleaded. "I can come before school, and after school, and at the weekends. Please?"

Jess grinned at her. "Thank you, Zoe. That would be great!" she replied. "You're so good at helping new animals feel at home here. In fact, your job could be to take special care of Sasha – if your mum doesn't mind."

"I don't mind at all," answered Lucy, smiling. "As long as you do all your homework first, Zoe. And you must do exactly as Jess tells you, especially when you're around the water."

Zoe nodded. She felt so proud – and so excited too! "Can I start this afternoon?" she asked hopefully.

"Of course! Just come and find me when you're home from school," Jess replied.

"Speaking of school, we'd better get you back to the cottage so you can have breakfast and put on your uniform," Lucy added.

 40

"And I must be off too," explained Great-Uncle Horace. He caught the look of disappointment on Zoe's face and added quickly, "Not for very long, I promise! But I've heard about some special swans a little bit further down the river and I'd love to see them. I'm going to sail my boat to where they're nesting. I'll be back at the zoo in a few days."

"And we've got a busy week ahead anyway, haven't we, Zoe?" Lucy added as Zoe ran to give Great-Uncle Horace a hug. "Come on now – let's go. I promise you can come back later!"

"See you soon!" called Zoe, waving at Jess as she and her mum jumped back into the Jeep. As they drove back towards the cottage, with Meep cuddled in Zoe's lap, Zoe felt a huge grin spreading across

 41

her face. She couldn't wait to spend more time with the gorgeous baby otters!

Chapter Four
Zoe's Special Visitors

"Mum, I'm home!" called Zoe, rushing into the cottage that afternoon. She had spent the whole day at school thinking about the baby otters and telling her friends and teacher about them. She was so excited about getting home and heading straight for their enclosure!

Zoe pulled her schoolbag off her

shoulders, but then noticed two pairs of shoes that she didn't recognise in the rack by the front door. There were some smart red high heels, and a small pair of sandals with a daisy pattern on them. *Of course — Auntie Carol and Olivia are here!* thought Zoe, smiling. *That's what Mum meant when she said we had a busy few days ahead. I'd completely forgotten that they were coming to stay!*

Hearing voices in the kitchen, Zoe ran through the door. Auntie Carol was sitting at the table with a cup of coffee, chatting with Lucy. She had dark hair cut in a short bob, and red glasses. Zoe's little cousin Olivia sat on her knee, her hair in pigtails, clutching a very threadbare teddy bear in her tiny hands. Meep was perched by the fruit bowl, sneakily helping himself to a banana.

"Zoe!" cried Auntie Carol, smiling. "How's my favourite niece? Olivia's been so excited about seeing you."

"Hi, Auntie Carol!" said Zoe, rushing over to hug them both. "Hi, Olivia. When did you get here?"

"At lunchtime," explained Auntie Carol. "And we seem to have picked a good week to come. Your mum's been telling us all about your new sea otters – how exciting! I hear you're going to be taking special care of the littlest one."

"I thought we could all walk over to the otter enclosure together, before tea," suggested Lucy.

"That would be great!" said Zoe. She grinned at her little cousin. "Do you like animals, Olivia?"

Olivia beamed back and nodded enthusiastically. Zoe thought she was *almost* as cute as the baby otters she'd met that morning, with her big blue eyes and smiley face. "I like Meep best!" Olivia told Zoe. "I want to hug him!"

Zoe giggled as Meep grumbled to himself. Olivia was only three years old, and the last time she and Auntie Carol had visited, she had squeezed poor Meep so tightly that he'd scampered upstairs to Zoe's bedroom and hidden under the bed until their visitors left.

Zoe quickly went to change out of her school uniform into jeans and a T-shirt, and then they all walked through the zoo together. Zoe and her mum pointed out different animals to Auntie Carol and Olivia along the way. "Those are the

emperor penguins.
Look at the
funny way they
waddle along!"
Zoe told her
little cousin, who
jumped up and
down excitedly, her
teddy still clutched
in her hands. "And

the giraffes are over there. Their necks are
really long, aren't they?"

"Eddie wants to see too," Olivia told
her, holding her teddy bear out.

Zoe took the teddy and lifted him up
high, as if to peer over the fence, before
returning him to Olivia. Auntie Carol and
Lucy chuckled. "I bought Eddie for Olivia
before she was even born," Auntie Carol

explained, nodding at the bear. "He's a
very special bear. He comes everywhere
with us – that's why he's a little bit
tattered!"

Jess was already inside the enclosure,
but instead of her normal zoo keeper's
uniform, she was dressed in a blue wetsuit.
She waved when she saw Zoe and Lucy
approaching. She was sitting on the

edge of the saltwater pool with her legs dangling in the water, watching Nina and Alex swim along together.

Jess reached into a bucket next to the pool, scooped up a handful of small silver fish and let them drop into the water. As the fish sank to the bottom of the pool, the twins rolled forward and plunged underwater, chasing after them.

"Look how good they are at diving for food," called Jess, smiling.

Zoe could tell that Olivia loved the gorgeous little otters. She was staring at them, her eyes wide and excited. Then Olivia caught sight of Sasha, perched on a rock at the edge of the pool, and gasped.

"That's Sasha! She's lovely, isn't she?" Zoe said.

"Can I hold her?" Olivia asked eagerly.

"Well, we don't usually pick up the wild animals because they aren't used to it and might not like it," Zoe explained gently. "Anyway, you're busy holding Eddie and you wouldn't want to put him down on the floor. He might get wet!"

Olivia nodded in agreement and gave Eddie a cuddle.

Zoe looked back at Sasha and thought she seemed a little bit sad. "Has Sasha tried diving for food yet?" she asked Jess, walking over to the pool.

"Not yet," replied Jess. "We'll need to bottle feed her for a bit longer, until she's a stronger swimmer and feels more at home here. We can definitely help her with her swimming though – in fact, now that you're here, we can give her a special lesson! First of all, you'll need this."

Jess reached behind her and pulled out a bag, tied with a ribbon. She passed it to Zoe, who opened it up carefully. "Your great-uncle asked me to buy it specially for you!" added Jess.

A thrill of excitement went through Zoe as she pulled out a ball of stretchy, shiny blue material. "A wetsuit, just like yours!"

she exclaimed, unrolling the material and holding up. "But it's the perfect size for me! Can I put it on now?"

"As long as your mum says it's OK?" said Jess, glancing at Lucy. "You've got some guests, haven't you?"

"No problem!" Lucy replied, smiling. "I bet your cousin would love to see your special suit, Zoe. What a lovely present, eh? I'll help you to put it on though.

52

Wetsuits can be really tricky if you're not used to them."

"You can get changed in the equipment room," said Jess, nodding to a small wooden hut at the edge of the enclosure. "I hope it fits!"

Inside the room, Zoe wriggled out of her clothes and pulled the wetsuit over her feet. "Actually, I think it's too small for me!" she gasped, struggling to squeeze the stretchy fabric over her legs. "I need a bigger size!"

"No, you don't! That's how wetsuits are supposed to fit, Zoe," Lucy explained as she helped Zoe wriggle into the rubbery suit. "They're always tight. That's how they keep you warm when you're spending lots of time in cold water. They trap a very thin layer of water between the suit and your body, which warms up and keeps you nice and toasty."

With a final wriggle from Zoe, Jess zipped up the back of the suit. "There, you're all ready!"

Zoe couldn't wait to get started. She was going to swim with three adorable baby otters! But when she stepped back outside the hut, she saw that Jess, Auntie Carol and Olivia had been joined by a new person in the enclosure – Mr Pinch, the grumpy zoo manager.

"What's going on?" Mr Pinch asked with a frown. "I heard that some new animals had arrived at the zoo, so I've come to make sure everything is under control. I didn't expect to see so many people here!"

"Oh, I hope we're not causing any

trouble," said Auntie Carol.

"Mr Pinch, this is my sister and my niece," Lucy explained. "They're just visiting the zoo for a few days and wanted to see the new arrivals."

"Well, I hope the children aren't getting underfoot," Mr Pinch muttered, throwing a grumpy glance at little Olivia. "If they make any mess, no doubt it will be left to me to clean it up!"

Zoe managed to hold her tongue, but she heard an angry chatter from Meep. Mr Pinch always grumbled about

Zoe wandering around the zoo, saying
that only *real* zoo keepers should work
with the animals, and not children. Zoe
thought this was very unfair, since she
always tried her best to help out. Still,
she never argued back. When Great-
Uncle Horace was away, Mr Pinch was
officially in charge of the zoo.

"Perhaps we'd better take Olivia back
to the cottage and find her a snack?"
suggested Lucy, and Auntie Carol nodded.
"We'll make a start on dinner too. But
Zoe does have a special job to do here,
Mr Pinch, so I hope you don't mind if she
stays for a little while."

"She'll be doing me a big favour,
Mr Pinch!" added Jess, smiling at Zoe.

Just then, the walkie-talkie attached
to Mr Pinch's uniform crackled. "Mr

Pinch, come in, please!" came the voice
of David, who worked in the elephant
enclosure. "There's a lady here from the
local paper, looking for you. She wants
to run a story about some of our newer
arrivals. Can you come and speak to
her?"

"Oh, very well. As if I'm not busy
enough!" Mr Pinch groaned, and
marched off in the direction of the
elephant enclosure.

"Phew!" chuckled Jess. "That should
keep Mr Pinch busy for a little while!"

Once Lucy and Auntie Carol had
taken Olivia back to the cottage, Zoe sat
down by the edge of the pool with Jess,
who showed her how to slowly ease her
legs into the water and get used to the
chilly temperature. Finally, Jess counted

to three and Zoe took a deep breath and jumped in. She was a good swimmer, but the cold water only came up to her chest so she could easily touch the bottom of the pool. As the cold water rushed inside her wetsuit, she kicked her legs hard to get warm. Immediately, Nina and Alex wriggled over to her, and Zoe laughed as they nuzzled up to her with their whiskery noses. She heard a little squeak behind her, turned and saw that Sasha was jumping in too!

"That's a good sign!" called Jess. "Sasha seems interested in you, Zoe – as soon as you got in the pool, she wanted to come swimming too! Stay close to her so she feels safe and supported. She might also like to try floating on her back."

Sasha paddled close to Zoe, her fur

sticking up in funny spikes and tufts. Zoe
started swimming slowly around the pool,
all the time checking that Sasha was still
with her. When Jess went to fetch some
toys for the otters to play with, Zoe took
the opportunity to whisper to the tiny

pup. "You're doing so well!" she said. "Do you want to try diving underwater?"

Sasha squealed in agreement and plunged her head under the surface, wriggling her body. But she couldn't get very far and quickly came back up, spluttering and squeaking crossly. "That's OK, Sasha. Every time you try it, you'll get better and better," Zoe reassured her.

Sasha squeaked again, hopefully this time, and nodded her little head at the plastic bucket on the side of the pool. "You want me to get you a fish?" repeated Zoe.

Right at that moment, Alex and Nina popped their heads out of the water, each of them holding a shiny silver fish in their teeth. Sasha gave a sad little wail. "Sasha, what's wrong?" Zoe asked anxiously. "Why are you so upset?"

Sasha nuzzled against Zoe for a cuddle and gave a tiny squeak. "Oh, Sasha! That's not true. Alex and Nina aren't better than you – they're just older," explained Zoe. "They've had much more time to practise swimming and diving. I promise you'll be able to do it just as easily as them, but you have to be a bit patient."

Sasha gave another sad squeak, and Zoe shook her head. "You shouldn't be embarrassed of your sticky-up fur!" she said. "I know Alex and Nina's fur is very soft and sleek, but I'll tell you a secret – I think yours is much nicer. It's a bit like my hair – look! My curls stick up too!"

But Sasha still seemed downhearted, and when Jess arrived back at the pool with her arms full of balls to play with, the little pup wriggled out of the pool and huddled down on a rock by herself. Zoe felt awful for her new friend. *I'm going to help Sasha in any way I can,* she thought to herself. *But how?*

Chapter Five
Mr Pinch's Plan

"But I don't *want* to go to bed!"

It was Tuesday evening and Zoe was helping Auntie Carol to get Olivia ready for bed – but it was turning out to be more difficult than Zoe had imagined! Olivia had put on her spotty pyjamas, drunk her cup of warm milk and brushed her teeth, but she did not want to go

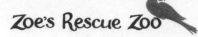
up to bed – no matter how hard Auntie
Carol and Zoe tried to persuade her.

"Zoe can stay up late! Why can't I?"
she complained, stamping her little feet on
the kitchen floor. "I'm a big girl too!"

Zoe held out her hand and smiled at
her little cousin. "Yes, you are! And when
you're even bigger, you'll be able to stay
up a bit later, like me. Come on, let's
go up to your bedroom together," she
suggested. "We can pick a story and I'll
read it to you! And Eddie can listen too,"
she added, picking up Olivia's tattered
teddy from the floor, where Olivia had
thrown him.

Olivia flung Eddie straight back down
again, only just missing Meep. Zoe tried
not to laugh as the little lemur scampered
quickly to the kitchen window and hid

behind the curtain, his cross little face peeping out. "I'm staying right here until Olivia goes to bed!" he squeaked firmly.

"I don't want a story!" grumbled Olivia. "I want to stay up!"

Auntie Carol sighed, but Zoe suddenly had an idea. "OK, Olivia!" she replied, smiling. "You can stay up. In fact, you're not allowed to go to bed! Not until you've played a special game with me. How does that sound?"

Olivia's face lit up and she nodded.

"First of all, you've got to do ten star jumps!" Zoe told her. "I'll count. Ready? One … two … three…"

Giggling, Olivia reached her hands up in the air and started jumping. "Next I want you to twirl around in a circle three times!" said Zoe. "Then tell me your ten favourite colours… And then do a roly-poly along the hallway carpet!"

Auntie Carol watched, chuckling, as Olivia followed Zoe's instructions, her tongue sticking out in concentration.

By the time she had touched her toes three times, the little girl was yawning sleepily, and seemed to have forgotten all about her tantrum earlier.

"Thanks, Zoe," whispered Auntie Carol as she carried Olivia upstairs to the spare bedroom. "That worked brilliantly!"

Once Olivia was sleeping, Zoe sat down at the kitchen table to eat dinner with her mum and Auntie Carol. As Lucy served the lasagne, she smiled at Zoe. "Jess tells me you're doing a fantastic job with the otters – especially Sasha. It sounds like they're settling in really well, just in time for the first special show."

"What show?" asked Zoe.

"Oh, I thought Jess would have mentioned it," said Lucy. "Well, this is all down to an idea Mr Pinch had last week."

Zoe pulled a face at the mention of the zoo manager. "Come on now, Zoe!" her mum went on. "I know Mr Pinch can be difficult sometimes, but this *is* a good idea. It's to help the zoo make a little bit more money. Every month, we'll choose a different animal to be the zoo's special focus. We'll put up posters, sell toys and books about those animals in the gift shop, and put on a show twice a day where the keeper tells the visitors all about that animal. Mr Pinch thought that the otters could be the first special animals, seeing as they're our newest arrivals. The first show's going to be in a few days' time."

Zoe had to admit that a special show sounded lovely – but she wondered if picking the otters first was such a good idea. Sasha was already finding it hard to keep up with the twins. How would she cope with a huge audience watching her?

On Thursday, Zoe raced home from school so that she could watch the very first show at the otter enclosure. Meep was waiting for her at the zoo entrance, perched on the carved wooden gates as usual.

"It's starting right now, Zoe!" he chirped eagerly.

Jess had put up signs directing visitors to the right place, showing a gorgeous

photograph of the new sea otters, and a
crowd was already gathering next to the
fence. Everyone was chatting eagerly.
"Aren't they lovely?" said one lady,
snapping a picture on her camera.

Zoe stood on her tiptoes to see better,
and Meep perched on her head. Nina
and Alex were splashing through their
saltwater pool, gliding on their backs
together, then racing to get the fish that
Jess threw into the water for them. Jess
was speaking into a special microphone
attached to her shirt collar, telling the
crowd all about the otters. "As you can
see, the twins love swimming!" she said.
"Sea otters love the water. In fact, in the
wild, sea otters can spend their whole
lives in the water. Imagine that!"

Zoe craned her neck to try to catch a

glimpse of the littlest otter. Sasha was
in the pool too, and doing her best to
keep up, but Zoe could see that she was
struggling. The pup was slower than the
twins, and couldn't reach any of the balls
or fish before them. Her tufty fur was

messy and spiky compared to their
sleek, shiny coats, and she seemed
to quickly grow tired from all the
swimming. Across the crowd,
Zoe saw Mr Pinch standing with
his arms crossed and a frown on
his face.

When Jess announced that the show was finished, the crowd all clapped and wandered off, talking eagerly about the gorgeous otters. Quickly, Zoe slipped inside the enclosure and rushed over to Sasha, who was sitting in a miserable furry huddle all by herself. When Sasha saw Zoe, she gave a sad squeak.

"It doesn't matter that you're not as quick as Nina and Alex yet," Zoe told her gently. "You're still doing really well!"

Nina and Alex swam up to their sister and squeaked encouragingly at her. "Your big brother and sister think so too, see?" said Zoe, smiling at the twins. "They're right – you just need a little bit more practice, and soon you'll be able to do everything they do. And we'll all help you!"

Nina squeaked in agreement and Alex nuzzled right up to Sasha. Zoe could tell that both of the older otters wanted to cheer their little sister up – and by the time she and Meep said goodbye to them all, Sasha *did* seem a bit happier. But as Zoe left the enclosure, she overheard Mr Pinch grumbling at Jess. "We need *all* the animals to be in good form," he muttered. "That little one can't keep up!"

Jess nodded reluctantly. "Well, she is younger than the twins. . ." she said.

"We have to keep the little otter out of the show until she's as big and strong as the others," Mr Pinch told her.

"Oh no," whispered Zoe to Meep as Mr Pinch marched off. "If Mr Pinch isn't going to let Sasha take part any more, she's going to be so upset!"

How would the little otter build her confidence if she wasn't allowed to take part in the show?

Chapter Six
Zoe's Training Tricks

After school on Friday, Zoe met Meep
at the gates and they ran straight to the
cottage. Auntie Carol and Olivia were
doing an animal jigsaw puzzle at the
kitchen table as they burst through the
door. "Hi, Zoe! How was school today?"
Auntie Carol called. "We've had such a
lovely day. Olivia met the llamas!"

"Oh, good!" replied Zoe, swapping her schoolbag for a small rucksack hanging on the back of the kitchen door. "I've just come home to grab my wetsuit," she explained, patting the rucksack. "I'm going to help Sasha."

"Good luck!" Auntie Carol smiled as Zoe dashed back outside.

Zoe and Meep raced to the otter enclosure, dodging through the busy crowds.

"Hi, Zoe!" called Jess from the saltwater pool. She was standing in the shallow end watching Nina and Alex swim. "Pop your wetsuit on and jump in!"

Zoe got changed in the equipment room. She was getting a bit more used to putting her wetsuit on now, though it was still tricky to wriggle into it! She put her hair up in a ponytail and joined Jess in the water. Nina and Alex splashed over to her and greeted her by nuzzling their whiskery noses against her body, and she gave them a cuddle back. "Where's Sasha?" she asked Jess.

There was a squeak as Sasha popped her head out from behind one of the wooden ramps that ran around the enclosure. "Sasha hasn't seemed very keen to get in the water today," Jess explained. "In fact, after her bottle of milk at lunchtime, she hasn't jumped into the pool once! I wondered if she might be tired – she's had a lot to take in over the last few days."

"Maybe she's feeling upset about how the show went last night," Zoe whispered to Meep, who was perched on a rock by the edge of the pool, taking care not to let any water splash his fur. Meep was friends with lots of water-loving animals, but he preferred to stay nice and dry! "Let's go and talk to her."

Zoe climbed out of the pool and went to sit with Sasha, who squeaked sadly at her. "What's wrong, Sasha?" Zoe asked. She listened as Sasha explained how things had changed since the otters had arrived at the zoo. When they'd been in the wild the twins had taken care of Sasha and caught fish for her but now they were too busy having fun and she felt really left out. When she was sure that Jess was distracted by Nina and Alex, Zoe said quietly, "Sasha, I need to tell you something. Mr Pinch thinks it might be better if just Nina and Alex perform in the next show."

The little otter gave another sad squeak.

"I know that makes you feel a bit sad," Zoe said, seeing the little pup's face fall and her big dark eyes widen. "But *I* know you can do everything your sister and brother can, with just a bit of practice. Why don't you come into the pool with me and have a swim?"

At first Sasha looked unsure, but eventually the little pup agreed. Zoe climbed back in the pool and waited for Sasha to splash in next to her. "Jess, would it be OK if I used one of these rings?" Zoe asked, nodding towards a stack of brightly coloured plastic rings on the side of the pool. "I want to see if Sasha would like to dive for it!"

"Of course, Zoe," said Jess, handing one over.

Zoe lifted up the ring, then let it drop from her hand and into the water. Sasha looked nervous, but rolled forward and plunged under.

Zoe crossed her fingers hopefully, but her heart sank as Sasha surfaced almost immediately, leaving the ring to sink right to the bottom of the pool. The little otter gave a frustrated squeal and shook her head. Zoe frowned as Sasha explained what the problem was. "You're worried you're going to get lost under the water?" she whispered back. "I promise that won't happen, Sasha – I'm here watching you the whole time! You've just lost your confidence, that's all. Let's try it again."

But Sasha was getting more and more upset – and to make matters worse, Nina and Alex had just caught some fish that Jess had thrown for them and were turning happy flips in the water to celebrate! Sasha gave a jealous, sulky squeak, turning her back on her big brother and sister.

Suddenly Zoe realised something. *This is just how Olivia was behaving last night when she wanted to stay up late like me! What if I distract Sasha with a fun game and see if that makes her feel happier?*

"Listen, Sasha," whispered Zoe, hoping her idea would work. "How would you like to eat a lovely shiny fish just like Nina and Alex?"

Sasha's eyes lit up and she nodded. "OK then!" replied Zoe. "You can have a fish – but you have to dive for it. We'll go right to the shallowest end of the water, and I'll stay with you the whole time, I promise."

Sasha hesitated, and Zoe could see the little pup thinking it through. She didn't want to try diving again, but she was eager to have a fish, like the twins! To

Zoe's delight, Sasha wriggled her furry little body to the shallowest part of the pool, where Zoe could kneel down in the water. Zoe grabbed a silver fish from the bucket at the side of the pool.

"I've got an idea! I'll count to three, and when you dive, I'll put my hand underwater too, and point to where the fish is," Zoe explained. "All you have to do is follow my hand! OK?"

Meep had scampered around the pool to sit closer to Zoe and Sasha. "And I'll cheer for you, Sasha!" the little lemur chirped warmly.

Sasha nodded but she looked really nervous.

"Ready?" said Zoe. "I'm going to drop the fish *now* – there it goes! And on the count of three, dive and follow my hand!

One … two … three!"

Sasha stuck her head under the water,
and gave a wriggle and a push. Zoe kept
her hand very close to the little otter's
head, so that Sasha could see it clearly
and be guided through the water. Down
they went, and just a moment later Sasha
caught the fish with her teeth. Quickly,
Zoe lifted her hand out of the water and
Sasha followed, popping up with a splash
and a triumphant squeal.

"You see?" said Zoe, smiling as Sasha
gobbled up the fish. "That wasn't so hard,
was it? I think you could give that one
more try, but this time we'll move to an
area of the pool that's a little bit deeper.
OK?"

The little pup was so excited that she'd
managed to catch the fish, she agreed

immediately. Zoe went and fetched
another fish then she took two steps
towards the deeper end and dropped it.
"One … two … three!" she said.

87

Sasha got to the fish even more quickly this time, following Zoe's hand right the way to the bottom of the pool. "Brilliant!" said Zoe, grinning. "You definitely earned that fish, Sasha. I knew you could do it!"

From the far side of the pool, Zoe heard clapping. Looking across, she saw that Jess was applauding! "Well done, Zoe!" she called. "You're doing so well. It's almost as though Sasha understands everything you're saying to her. Maybe the sound of your voice is soothing her. Either way, it's working!"

Grinning to herself, Zoe clambered out of the pool and scooped up another tiny silver fish from the bucket, which she held out for Sasha. The little pup gobbled it down, her eyes wide with excitement.

Zoe smiled at the little otter pup. "We'll

do some more swimming tomorrow and I promise you can have some more fish then," she whispered to Sasha.

Meep sighed. "Seeing Sasha enjoying a snack is making me feel peckish!"

Zoe giggled. Meep was *always* hungry! As she walked home for tea with the little lemur perched on her shoulder, Zoe felt tired but happy. "I really think little Sasha's doing much better now, don't you?" she said, reaching up to tickle Meep's fluffy belly.

Meep squeaked in agreement, though Zoe could tell he was already distracted by the thought of tea. She was pleased she could help the young sea otter, even if she couldn't take part in the show yet...

"Remember, today's show starts at three o'clock!" Zoe reminded her mum as she laced up her trainers.

"I wouldn't miss it for anything, Zoe. Auntie Carol and Olivia will be there too," Lucy promised.

It was Saturday, and Zoe was setting off to help Jess get the sea otter enclosure ready for the show. She'd been kept busy all morning with her homework, then feeding the monkeys and the hippos their breakfast, but now that the show was almost here she was feeling jittery and nervous. She knew that Nina and Alex would perform brilliantly for the crowd — but she was worried that Sasha might still get upset seeing her big brother and sister being the stars, when she wasn't even allowed to take part. *If she does get upset today, at least Meep and I will be there to cheer her up*, she told herself.

Jess was sweeping inside the enclosure when Zoe arrived and used her special necklace to open the gate. "Zoe, if you could grab that spare broom and help me finish this off, that would be amazing!" she called. "Then we'll need to stock up on fresh fish and check the saltwater levels and temperature of the pool ready for the show. Mr Pinch will be coming along to watch again today. It'll be great to show him how well the otters are getting on!"

Zoe got stuck in straight away. There were always plenty of jobs to help out with at the Rescue Zoo, and she loved being involved – even if it was hard work sometimes! Jess was humming cheerfully as they completed their tasks, and Zoe found herself joining in. She was even happier to see Sasha splashing in the water with her brother and sister, following them when they dived, even though she couldn't manage to swim as deeply as they could. "I think our practice yesterday really helped Sasha!" she said to Jess.

The keeper smiled. "Yes, she's doing so much better today, isn't she?"

Zoe saw Sasha's little ears prick up.

Eagerly, the little pup paddled towards the edge of the pool and squeaked up hopefully to Zoe.

Zoe's heart sank. The little otter was asking if she'd be able to take part in today's show – but Zoe knew she couldn't. She felt sure that Mr Pinch wouldn't have changed his mind.

When Jess was busy in the equipment room, Zoe found a moment to crouch down next to the pool and speak to Sasha. "I'm sorry, Sasha," she said gently. "You're doing really well, like Jess said, but Nina and Alex will do this show by themselves, and hopefully you can join in next time?"

As Sasha's face fell, Nina and Alex squeaked kindly and encouragingly at their little sister, telling her not to be

upset or worried. Zoe bent down and
scooped the tiny otter out of the water,
and wrapped her in a big, fluffy towel to
warm her up. "Let's get you dry, and then
we can pick a nice spot on the rocks to
sit and watch the show,"
she suggested quietly.
"Even if you can't
be in it, you can
still enjoy it!
And you'll
be able to
have a good
look at
everybody
in the crowd
– I always
think that's lots
of fun."

By the time the crowd started to assemble on the other side of the fence, the enclosure was looking spick and span, with a bucket full of fresh fish by the water's edge. Jess had attached the special microphone to her shirt and the twins were gliding through the water together. Zoe sat with Sasha curled up next to her and Meep perched on her shoulder. "Look, there's your mum and Auntie Carol and Olivia – and Great-Uncle Horace!" the little lemur squeaked.

Zoe smiled and waved as her family took their places next to the fence, Olivia clutching her tattered teddy. "Great-Uncle Horace, you're back!" she called. "Did you find the special swans you were looking for?"

Great-Uncle Horace was beaming.

Zoe's Rescue Zoo

"I did!" he called. "Wonderful, elegant
creatures! But I'm absolutely thrilled to
be home in time to watch our newest
arrivals in action. I hear you've been
doing a splendid job here, Zoe!"

Just then they heard Jess's voice come
over the loudspeakers.

"I think it's time to start!" she
announced, holding up the first bright-
yellow ball. "Thank you for coming,
everyone. I'm very happy to introduce
twins Nina and Alex, who are a year
old. They are our newest animals at the
Rescue Zoo so please give them a warm
welcome!"

The crowd chattered excitedly as
the otters began swooping and diving,
chasing after the fish and turning
somersaults. Zoe glanced over at the

96

audience and grinned to see Auntie Carol
lifting a wide-eyed Olivia right up to
the fence so that she could see better. The
little girl chuckled and pointed as the
baby otters tumbled through the water.

I wish Sasha could have taken part, thought
Zoe, looking down at the tufty little otter
sitting beside her, *but at least everyone's
enjoying the show – and this time there's
nothing for Mr Pinch to get cross about!*

Suddenly Zoe heard a familiar, anxious
wail from the crowd. "Eddie!"

She looked over again and saw Olivia
reaching desperately over the side of the
fence. "Mummy, I dropped Eddie in the
water!" she whimpered, tears beginning
to stream down her face.

Zoe peered into the deepest part of the
pool, right by the fence. She could just

make out a blurry shape, sinking deeper and deeper: Olivia's precious teddy bear, Eddie. Olivia started to cry louder, and there was a murmur throughout the crowd. Zoe heard Mr Pinch grumble, "What is going on?"

Then Zoe noticed a sudden movement from next to her – a fuzzy blur shuffled quickly towards the pool and leapt in with a little splash. Zoe realised what was happening, just as a man in the crowd called out, "Look! There's another baby otter – an even smaller one!"

Chapter Seven
Sasha Saves the Day!

"Sasha!" cried Zoe. The little pup had
scampered down from her seat and
splashed into the pool! The crowd gasped,
and Zoe held her breath as Sasha glided
through the water. She swam right
past where her brother and sister were
performing and disappeared under the
surface with a wriggle and a splash.

A moment later her tufty head popped back up, dripping with water and with fur sticking up everywhere. Her black eyes gleamed happily as she showed the crowd what she was carrying in her teeth.

"Eddie!" yelled Olivia. "She's got Eddie!"

Sasha swam to the side of the pool with a very soggy teddy bear, and Jess bent down and gently took Eddie from her. She gave him a careful squeeze so that most of the water trickled out, and then leaned over the fence and handed him back to Olivia, who hugged him tight. "Eddie!"

Suddenly the whole crowd was laughing and cheering, chattering about the clever little otter, and snapping pictures. "That has to be the cutest thing I've ever seen!"

Zoe heard a teenage girl with long red hair tell her friend. "A gorgeous baby otter, rescuing a teddy bear!"

"I filmed it all on my phone!" her friend told her. "I can't wait to show everyone at school. They'll all want to come and see her!"

Zoe glanced over at Mr Pinch. The grumpy zoo manager's expression had changed completely. He was beaming from ear to ear and nodding along with the rest of the crowd. "Of course, this special show was all my idea," he explained loudly to whoever would listen. "And it was my decision to feature *all* of the sea otters too. Very intelligent creatures. I just knew they'd be popular!"

"Zoe, look!" chirped Meep, pointing. "All the otters are swimming together!"

Zoe turned back to the pool – and grinned. Nina and Alex had both offered their little sister a furry paw, and all three were floating along on their backs, with Sasha in the middle. From the cheerful squeals and squeaks she was letting out, Zoe could tell she was very happy. Eagerly, she tried a somersault in the water — and although she didn't quite manage it, and splashed water everywhere, the crowd seemed to love it. "They are all so adorable!" cried a blonde lady standing close to Mr Pinch. "The scruffy little one is the cutest. I'd come back and watch her every day if I could."

"I can't believe it," whispered Zoe to Meep. "Sasha is the star of the whole show!"

When the show was over and the audience began trickling away, Zoe ran to give her mum and Great-Uncle

Horace a hug before they went back to the cottage. "You did such a good job of helping Sasha gain her confidence, Zoe," said Lucy, smiling. "I'm so proud of you."

"Hear, hear!" said Great-Uncle Horace.

Zoe shook her head. "It was all down to Sasha – and to Olivia!" she added, beaming at her little cousin, who giggled. "And to Eddie, of course!" and she patted the soggy teddy bear on the head.

"We'll have a special tea tonight, to celebrate," said Lucy. "You'll come too, won't you, Uncle Horace?"

"Can I stay here for a little bit longer?" asked Zoe. "I want to help Jess finish tidying up. I'll be home soon!"

Lucy agreed, and Zoe waved them off. Then she knelt by the side of the pool to talk to the youngest sea otter.

106

"Sasha, you were amazing!" she whispered. "You rescued Olivia's special teddy and you swam in front of everyone, just like Nina and Alex!"

Sasha nodded and squeaked back, her eyes bright. "I'm so glad you're feeling more confident," Zoe replied, smiling.

As Zoe and Meep left the enclosure a little bit later, Zoe turned back to glance over the fence one last time, and grinned. The three otters were in the pool, all of them clasping paws again as they floated through the water. "Sasha seems really happy now, doesn't she, Meep?" Zoe said.

"So do Nina and Alex," chirped Meep. "And *I'm* really happy they've come to live at the Rescue Zoo with us, Zoe!"

"Me too, Meep," replied Zoe, cuddling her little friend. "I wonder what animal Great-Uncle Horace will bring home with him next time? I can't wait to find out!"

If you enjoyed Sasha's story,
look out for:

Zoe's Rescue ZOO

The Eager Elephant

Chapter One
Meep Gets into Mischief

Zoe Parker wrinkled her nose and squeezed her eyes tightly shut. "Aaaa-chooo!" she sneezed as dust went up her nose. "Aaaa-chooo!"

Zoe was raking up the minty-smelling leaves in the koala enclosure at the Rescue Zoo. All around her, tall green trees stretched up from the dusty, pebbly ground. Every time Zoe moved her rake, a small cloud of dust puffed into the air – and straight up her nose!

As the branches above her head shook, Zoe glanced up. Perched in the tree was Matilda, one of the koalas. Zoe thought she was one of the cuddliest animals at the Rescue Zoo, with her soft grey fur, cute black nose and big fluffy ears. But right now Matilda didn't look at all cuddly – she looked cross!

The koala gave a noisy chatter, and a tiny creature scampered out of the leaves and shot down the tree trunk. He stuck his pink tongue out at Matilda before leaping on to Zoe's shoulder.

"Meep!" Zoe said, grinning at the little mouse lemur. Meep was her very best friend. He was so small he could easily ride on Zoe's shoulder, and he was *always* getting into mischief!

The koala chattered again crossly, and Zoe looked up in time to see her fluffy bottom disappear further up the tree. Zoe giggled. Being with all the animals was her favourite thing about her zoo home, even when they were cross!

Zoe was very lucky – because she *lived* at the Rescue Zoo! Her Great-Uncle Horace was the zoo owner, and knew almost everything about animals. Zoe didn't see him very often, because he spent lots of time travelling around the world, looking for animals that needed help. Whenever he found an animal in trouble or without a home he brought them back to live at the Rescue Zoo! Zoe's mum, Lucy, was the zoo vet, and she and Zoe lived in a cottage on the edge of the zoo.

Matilda shook her furry head and chattered crossly again at Meep, and Zoe smiled. "You're right, Matilda," she replied. "Meep is the naughtiest lemur I've ever met, too."

Living at the Rescue Zoo was the first exciting thing about Zoe, but the second thing was *even* more special. Zoe knew a very big secret: animals can understand what people say, and talk to them all the time! But only a few lucky people can talk back to them. Zoe was one of these special people. Ever since her sixth birthday she had understood every growl, grunt, squeak and roar the animals made! But she could never tell anyone the animals' secret – not even her family.

"What were you doing this time, Meep?" said Zoe as the lemur snuggled into her shoulder.

"I wasn't doing anything naughty, Zoe," Meep complained grumpily. "I just wanted to try one of Matilda's special leaves. They look so green and juicy, and they smell so nice. But I had one tiny bite and then I spat it straight out. It tasted horrible!"

"Oh, Meep!" Zoe sighed. "Those are eucalyptus leaves, and they're poisonous to most animals! They would have made you *very* sick. Matilda can eat them because koalas have special tummies that protect them. She was just trying to help you." She smiled up at Matilda. "Thank you," she told the koala gratefully. "No wonder you were upset with cheeky

Meep!"

Matilda nodded her furry head and quickly chattered back.

"No, I'm sure he won't do it again!" Zoe replied. "Will you, Meep?"

Meep's big golden eyes were wide as he shook his head. "I'll stick to bananas from now on. And apples. And maybe nuts too . . . and sunflower seeds. . ."

Zoe giggled as Meep started listing all the foods he liked. Meep was a little animal with a big appetite!

Up in the tree, Matilda suddenly gave an excited squeak and began chattering eagerly.

"What is it?" Zoe asked curiously.

"Let's go and see!" chirped Meep, bounding nimbly back up the tree. Zoe quickly grabbed the lowest branches and pulled herself up to where Matilda was sitting. She wasn't as good at climbing as the koalas, or Meep, but she was still the best in her class. She had lots of practice playing with her animal friends!

Peering through the leaves over the top of the wooded enclosure, Zoe saw a bright-yellow jeep rumbling slowly through the zoo gates. It was very dusty, with big muddy wheels, and looked like it had travelled a long way. The back of the jeep was open and flat, without a roof or any seats, and a large wooden crate was strapped on to it.

Around her, Zoe heard lots of noise as the other zoo animals spotted the jeep. The grizzly bears growled curiously. The turtles swam to the edge of their lagoon enclosure. And Oscar, the friendly African elephant, lifted his big trunk in the air and gave a noisy trumpet.

As the jeep got closer, Zoe could see something through the dirt on the door. There was a familiar logo painted there – a hot-air balloon, the symbol of the Rescue Zoo! Zoe's heart gave a big thump of excitement. "It's Great-Uncle Horace!" she gasped. "He's back from his safari trip. And he's brought a new animal for the Rescue Zoo!"

Look out for more amazing animal adventures at the Rescue Zoo!

The Rescue Princesses

Have you read them all?

nosy crow